400+ Cool & Unbelievable Invention Facts for Kids

Contents

Introduction	4
Chapter 1: The history of the wheel	5
Chapter 2: The invention of the telephone	8
Chapter 3: The story behind the first airplane	12
Chapter 4: The creation of the internet	15
Chapter 5: The invention of the printing press	18
Chapter 6: The development of the television	25
Chapter 7: The origin of the bicycle	28
Chapter 8: The invention of the light bulb	32
Chapter 9: The history of the computer	35
Chapter 10: The creation of the steam engine	39
Chapter 11: The invention of the camera	43
Chapter 12: The development of the automobile	47
Chapter 13: The story behind the first robot	51
Chapter 14: The invention of the microscope	55
Chapter 15: The creation of the refrigerator	60
Chapter 16: The invention of the calculator	64
Chapter 17: The development of the compass	68
Chapter 18: The story behind the first hot air balloon	72
Chapter 19: The invention of the sewing machine	76

Chapter 20: The creation of the telescope	81
Chapter 21: The invention of the microwave oven	85
Chapter 22: The development of the electric motor	89
Chapter 23: The story behind the first submarine	93
Chapter 24: The invention of the radio	97
Chapter 25: The creation of the rocket	101
Conclusion	106

Introduction

Get ready to blast off on an incredible journey through time and space! In this amazing book, ""400+ Cool & Unbelievable Invention Facts for Kids,"" you'll discover the fascinating stories behind some of the most groundbreaking inventions in human history. From the humble wheel to the mighty rocket, these inventions have transformed the way we live, work, and explore the world around us.

Did you know that the first wheels were made of stone and used as potter's wheels in ancient Mesopotamia? Or that the first successful airplane was made of wood, fabric, and metal, and flew for just 12 seconds? These are just a few of the mind-blowing facts you'll learn as you dive into the pages of this book.

But that's not all! You'll also explore the creation of the internet, the development of the telephone, the invention of the light bulb, and so much more. Each topic is brought to life with engaging stories that will spark your imagination and make you wonder what other incredible inventions the future might hold.

So buckle up and get ready for an adventure like no other. Whether you're a budding inventor, a curious kid, or just someone who loves to learn, this book has something for everyone. With over 400 amazing facts and stories, you'll never look at the world around you the same way again. Let's get started!

Chapter 1: The history of the wheel

1. The first wheels were made of stone and used as potter's wheels in Mesopotamia around 3500 BCE.

2. The oldest known wheel and axle mechanism was discovered in Slovenia, dating back to 3200 BCE.

3. The Egyptians invented the spoked wheel around 2000 BCE, which made chariots faster and lighter.

4. The Greeks and Romans improved wheel technology by using iron rims and hubs, making them more durable.

5. The Celts, around 1000 BCE, invented the iron tire, which provided better traction and stability for wheels.

6. The Chinese invented the wheelbarrow around 100 BCE, revolutionizing transportation and agriculture.

7. The Romans built an extensive network of roads, some of which still exist today, thanks to wheeled vehicles.

8. The waterwheel, invented by the Greeks around 400 BCE, harnessed the power of water for milling and irrigation.

9. The Medieval period saw the invention of the spinning wheel, which greatly improved textile production.

10. Leonardo da Vinci designed a helicopter-like machine in the 15th century, featuring a rotating spiral "wheel."

11. The invention of the Falkirk Wheel in 2002 allowed boats to be lifted between canals at different heights.

12. The Segway, invented in 2001, is a two-wheeled, self-balancing electric vehicle that revolutionized personal transportation.

13. The modern car wheel has evolved to include rubber tires, air-filled inner tubes, and sophisticated suspension systems.

14. The invention of the Ferris Wheel by George Washington Gale Ferris Jr. in 1893 introduced a new form of amusement ride.

15. The Cyr Wheel, invented by Daniel Cyr in 2003, is a large metal wheel used in acrobatic performances.

16. The invention of the wheelchair has provided mobility and independence to millions of people with disabilities worldwide.

17. The London Eye, a giant Ferris wheel, offers breathtaking views of the city and is a popular tourist attraction.

18. The High Roller in Las Vegas is currently the tallest Ferris wheel in the world, standing at 550 feet tall.

19. The invention of the pulley, which incorporates a wheel, has been used for thousands of years to lift heavy objects.

20. NASA's Mars rovers, Spirit and Opportunity, used specially designed wheels to navigate the rough Martian terrain.

Chapter 2: The invention of the telephone

1. In 1876, Alexander Graham Bell invented the telephone, a device that would change the world by allowing people to talk to each other over long distances.

2. Bell's first successful telephone call was to his assistant, Thomas Watson, who was in another room. Bell said, "Mr. Watson, come here, I want to see you!"

3. The telephone quickly became popular, and by 1900, there were over 1.5 million telephones in use in the United States alone.

4. Bell's telephone worked by converting sound waves into electrical signals, which were then transmitted over a wire to the receiver on the other end.

5. The first telephone exchange, which allowed multiple telephones to be connected, was established in New Haven, Connecticut, in 1878.

6. In 1915, the first transcontinental telephone call was made, connecting people from New York to San Francisco, a distance of over 3,000 miles.

7. The first transatlantic telephone cable was laid in 1956, enabling telephone communication between Europe and North America.

8. The invention of the rotary dial in the early 1900s made it easier for people to make telephone calls without the help of an operator.

9. In 1973, Martin Cooper of Motorola made the first handheld cellular phone call, paving the way for the mobile phones we use today.

10. The telephone has been instrumental in connecting people during emergencies, such as hurricanes, earthquakes, and other natural disasters.

11. The telephone has also been used for important historical events, such as President John F. Kennedy's "Hotline" to the Soviet Union during the Cold War.

12. In 1984, the breakup of the Bell System led to increased competition in the telephone industry and the introduction of new technologies and services.

13. The invention of the answering machine in the 1960s allowed people to leave messages when the person they were calling was unavailable.

14. The telephone has been used in countless movies, TV shows, and books as a plot device to create suspense, convey important information, or connect characters.

15. The telephone has also been used for less serious purposes, such as prank calls and telemarketing, which can be annoying or even harmful.

16. The invention of the speakerphone in the 1970s made it possible for multiple people to participate in a telephone conversation at the same time.

17. The rise of Voice over Internet Protocol (VoIP) technology in the early 2000s allowed people to make telephone calls over the internet, often at a lower cost than traditional telephone service.

18. The telephone has been adapted for use by people with disabilities, such as those who are deaf or hard of hearing, through devices like TTY (teletypewriter) and video relay services.

19. The telephone has also been used for education, such as distance learning programs that allow students to participate in classes remotely.

20. Today, the telephone remains an essential tool for communication, connecting people across the globe and enabling them to share ideas, experiences, and information instantly.

Chapter 3: The story behind the first airplane

1. In 1903, brothers Wilbur and Orville Wright invented the first successful airplane, which they called the Wright Flyer.

2. The Wright brothers had been interested in flying since childhood and spent years experimenting with kites, gliders, and other flying machines.

3. To power their airplane, the Wright brothers built a lightweight gasoline engine that produced 12 horsepower.

4. The Wright Flyer was made of wood, fabric, and metal and had a wingspan of 40 feet and a weight of 750 pounds.

5. On December 17, 1903, at Kitty Hawk, North Carolina, Orville Wright piloted the first successful flight, which lasted 12 seconds and covered 120 feet.

6. The Wright brothers made three more flights that day, with Wilbur Wright piloting the longest flight, which lasted 59 seconds and covered 852 feet.

7. News of the Wright brothers' successful flights spread quickly, and they became famous overnight.

8. The Wright brothers continued to improve their airplane design and made many more successful flights in the following years.

9. In 1908, Wilbur Wright made the first public flight in France, amazing spectators and silencing critics who had doubted their claims.

10. The Wright brothers' invention of the airplane paved the way for the development of commercial aviation and changed the way people travel forever.

11. The Wright Flyer was powered by two propellers, which were spun in opposite directions to provide stability and prevent the airplane from spinning out of control.

12. The Wright brothers used a special technique called "wing-warping" to control the direction of their airplane, which involved twisting the wings to change their shape.

13. The Wright brothers faced many challenges and setbacks in their quest to invent the airplane, including crashes and engine failures.

14. The Wright brothers were skilled mechanics and built their own wind tunnel to test their airplane designs.

15. The Wright Flyer had a special cradle that allowed the pilot to lie on his stomach and control the airplane with his hands and feet.

16. The Wright brothers' first successful flight was witnessed by only a handful of people, including several lifeguards from a nearby lifesaving station.

17. The Wright brothers' airplane was later donated to the Smithsonian Institution in Washington, D.C., where it remains on display today.

18. The invention of the airplane had a profound impact on society, changing the way people travel, conduct business, and wage war.

19. The Wright brothers' legacy lives on today, with airports, museums, and monuments named in their honor around the world.

20. The Wright brothers' invention of the airplane is considered one of the greatest achievements in the history of science and technology.

Chapter 4: The creation of the internet

1. The internet began in the 1960s as a project called ARPANET, which was funded by the United States Department of Defense.

2. The first message sent over the ARPANET was "LOGIN," but the system crashed after only the first two letters were transmitted.

3. In 1971, Ray Tomlinson invented email, which allowed people to send electronic messages to each other over the ARPANET.

4. In 1973, Vint Cerf and Bob Kahn developed the Transmission Control Protocol/Internet Protocol (TCP/IP), which became the standard for communication between computers on the internet.

5. In 1983, the Domain Name System (DNS) was created, which allowed people to use easy-to-remember names for websites instead of numerical IP addresses.

6. In 1990, Tim Berners-Lee invented the World Wide Web, which made it possible for people to access information on the internet using web browsers.

7. The first web browser, called WorldWideWeb, was also created by Tim Berners-Lee and was released in 1991.

8. In 1993, the first web browser for the general public, called Mosaic, was released by Marc Andreessen and Eric Bina.

9. The first online shopping transaction took place in 1994, when a man sold a CD to his friend over the internet using a credit card.

10. In 1995, Amazon.com was founded by Jeff Bezos and became one of the first successful online retailers.

11. In 1998, Google was founded by Larry Page and Sergey Brin and quickly became the most popular search engine on the internet.

12. In 1999, the first successful online music store, Napster, was launched, allowing people to share music files over the internet.

13. In 2001, Wikipedia was launched, providing a free online encyclopedia that anyone could edit and contribute to.

14. In 2004, Facebook was founded by Mark Zuckerberg and quickly became the most popular social networking site in the world.

15. In 2005, YouTube was founded by Chad Hurley, Steve Chen, and Jawed Karim, allowing people to upload and share videos online.

16. In 2006, Twitter was launched, providing a platform for people to share short messages and updates with their followers.

17. In 2007, the iPhone was released by Apple, which made it possible for people to access the internet on their mobile phones.

18. In 2008, Airbnb was founded, allowing people to rent out their homes or apartments to travelers over the internet.

19. In 2009, the digital currency Bitcoin was created by an anonymous person or group using the name Satoshi Nakamoto.

20. Today, the internet has become an essential part of our daily lives, connecting people and businesses around the world and providing access to a vast array of information and services.

Chapter 5: The invention of the printing press

1. In the 15th century, books were very expensive and rare because they had to be copied by hand. This all changed when Johannes Gutenberg invented the printing press around 1440. Gutenberg's printing press used movable metal type, which allowed books to be printed much faster and cheaper than ever before. This invention revolutionized the way knowledge was shared and made books available to many more people.

2. Gutenberg's first printed book was the Bible, which took about three years to complete. The Gutenberg Bible was a beautiful work of art, with 42 lines of text per page and colorful illustrations. Only about 180 copies were printed, and they were sold for the equivalent of three years' wages for an average clerk. Today, only 49 copies of the Gutenberg Bible still exist, and they are some of the most valuable books in the world.

3. The printing press spread quickly throughout Europe, and by the end of the 15th century, there were printing presses in over 200 cities. This allowed for the rapid spread of new ideas and knowledge, which helped to fuel the Renaissance and the Scientific Revolution. Many famous works, such as the plays of

Shakespeare and the works of Galileo, were printed during this time.

4. The printing press also played a key role in the Protestant Reformation, which began in 1517 when Martin Luther nailed his 95 Theses to the door of a church in Germany. Luther's ideas were quickly printed and distributed throughout Europe, allowing them to spread far and wide. This helped to spark a religious revolution that challenged the authority of the Catholic Church and led to the creation of new Protestant denominations.

5. The printing press also had a profound impact on education. Before the printing press, books were so expensive that only the wealthy could afford them. With the advent of the printing press, books became more affordable and accessible, which allowed for the spread of literacy and learning. Universities and schools began to use printed textbooks, and libraries were established to house the growing number of books.

6. The printing press also played a role in the development of newspapers and magazines. The first newspaper was published in Germany in 1605, and by the 18th century, newspapers were being printed in many countries around the world. Magazines also began to appear, covering topics such as fashion, politics, and science.

These publications helped to keep people informed about current events and new ideas.

7. The printing press also had an impact on the way governments communicated with their citizens. Governments began to use the printing press to publish laws, proclamations, and other official documents. This allowed for greater transparency and accountability in government, as citizens could now read and understand the laws that governed them.

8. The printing press also played a role in the development of the modern novel. Before the printing press, most books were religious or scholarly works. With the advent of the printing press, authors began to write books for entertainment, such as novels and plays. This helped to create a new genre of literature that is still popular today.

9. The printing press also had an impact on the way music was shared and enjoyed. Before the printing press, music was usually passed down orally or through handwritten manuscripts. With the advent of the printing press, sheet music could be printed and distributed, allowing for the wider spread of musical compositions. This helped to create a new industry of music publishing and allowed for the development of new musical styles and genres.

10. The printing press also played a role in the development of the modern map. Before the printing press, maps were usually hand-drawn and very expensive. With the advent of the printing press, maps could be printed and distributed more easily, allowing for greater accuracy and detail. This helped to fuel the Age of Exploration, as explorers used printed maps to navigate the world and claim new territories.

11. The printing press also had an impact on the way art was created and enjoyed. Before the printing press, art was usually created for wealthy patrons or religious purposes. With the advent of the printing press, artists could create prints of their work, which could be sold to a wider audience. This helped to democratize art and allowed for the development of new artistic styles and movements.

12. The printing press also played a role in the development of the modern calendar. Before the printing press, calendars were usually handwritten and only available to a select few. With the advent of the printing press, calendars could be printed and distributed more widely, allowing for greater standardization and accuracy. This helped to create a more unified sense of time and allowed for better planning and organization.

13. The printing press also had an impact on the way science was conducted and shared. Before the printing press, scientific ideas were usually shared through letters or lectures. With the advent of the printing press, scientific papers and books could be printed and distributed more widely, allowing for greater collaboration and peer review. This helped to accelerate scientific progress and led to many important discoveries and inventions.

14. The printing press also played a role in the development of the modern encyclopedia. Before the printing press, encyclopedias were usually handwritten and only available to a select few. With the advent of the printing press, encyclopedias could be printed and distributed more widely, allowing for greater access to knowledge. The first printed encyclopedia was published in 1501, and many more followed in the centuries that followed.

15. The printing press also had an impact on the way religion was practiced and shared. Before the printing press, religious texts were usually handwritten and only available to clergy and scholars. With the advent of the printing press, religious texts could be printed and distributed more widely, allowing for greater access and interpretation. This helped to fuel religious movements and reforms, such as the Protestant Reformation.

16. The printing press also played a role in the development of the modern dictionary. Before the printing press, dictionaries were usually handwritten and only available to a select few. With the advent of the printing press, dictionaries could be printed and distributed more widely, allowing for greater standardization and accuracy of language. The first printed dictionary was published in 1538, and many more followed in the centuries that followed.

17. The printing press also had an impact on the way politics was conducted and shared. Before the printing press, political ideas were usually shared through speeches or pamphlets. With the advent of the printing press, political tracts and manifestos could be printed and distributed more widely, allowing for greater public participation and debate. This helped to fuel political revolutions and reforms, such as the American and French Revolutions.

18. The printing press also played a role in the development of the modern comic book. Before the printing press, comics were usually hand-drawn and only available to a select few. With the advent of the printing press, comics could be printed and distributed more widely, allowing for greater access and enjoyment. The first comic book was published in 1933, and the genre has continued to evolve and grow in popularity ever since.

19. The printing press also had an impact on the way advertising was conducted and shared. Before the printing press, advertising was usually done through word of mouth or signage. With the advent of the printing press, advertisements could be printed and distributed more widely, allowing for greater reach and effectiveness. This helped to create a new industry of advertising and marketing, which has continued to grow and evolve over the centuries.

20. Today, the impact of the printing press can still be felt in many aspects of our lives. Although digital technologies have largely replaced the printing press, the ability to share ideas and information quickly and widely remains a key part of our society. From books and newspapers to social media and online platforms, the legacy of the printing press lives on, continuing to shape the way we communicate and learn.

Chapter 6: The development of the television

1. In the late 1800s, a young inventor named Paul Nipkow created a spinning disk with holes that could scan images, laying the groundwork for television.

2. In 1927, Philo Farnsworth, a 21-year-old inventor, successfully transmitted the first electronic television image, which was a simple line.

3. RCA, a major electronics company, hired a Russian immigrant named Vladimir Zworykin to develop television technology in the 1920s and 1930s.

4. The first public television broadcast in the United States took place at the 1939 World's Fair in New York City.

5. During World War II, television development was put on hold as resources were redirected to the war effort.

6. In 1946, the first television sets went on sale to the public, but they were very expensive and had small screens.

7. The first television show ever broadcast was a variety show called "The Queen's Messenger" in 1928.

8. In the 1950s, television became more affordable and popular, with the rise of shows like "I Love Lucy" and "The Ed Sullivan Show."

9. The first color television sets were sold in the 1950s, but it took several years for color programming to become widely available.

10. In 1962, the first satellite television signal was transmitted across the Atlantic Ocean, paving the way for global television.

11. The first television remote control, called the "Lazy Bones," was introduced in 1950 and was connected to the TV by a wire.

12. In 1969, Neil Armstrong's first steps on the moon were watched by an estimated 650 million people around the world on television.

13. The first video game console that could be connected to a television, the Magnavox Odyssey, was released in 1972.

14. In the 1980s, cable television and VCRs became popular, allowing people to watch a wider variety of shows and movies at home.

15. The first flat-screen plasma TV was introduced by Fujitsu in 1997, revolutionizing the design and size of televisions.

16. In the early 2000s, the rise of high-definition television (HDTV) brought a new level of picture quality to television screens.

17. Smart TVs, which can connect to the internet and run apps, became popular in the 2010s, blurring the line between television and computers.

18. Streaming services like Netflix and Hulu have changed the way people watch television, allowing them to watch shows on-demand.

19. In 2020, during the COVID-19 pandemic, television played a crucial role in keeping people informed and entertained while they stayed at home.

20. Today, television continues to evolve with new technologies like 4K resolution, HDR, and virtual reality, promising an even more immersive viewing experience in the future.

Chapter 7: The origin of the bicycle

1. The first known bicycle-like invention was the "running machine" created by German inventor Karl Drais in 1817. It had no pedals and was propelled by the rider's feet pushing against the ground.

2. In 1839, Scottish blacksmith Kirkpatrick Macmillan invented the first pedal-driven bicycle. However, his invention didn't gain much popularity during his lifetime.

3. The French inventor Pierre Michaux and his son Ernest are often credited with creating the first mass-produced bicycle, the "velocipede," in the 1860s.

4. The velocipede, also known as the "boneshaker," had wooden wheels with iron tires and was very uncomfortable to ride on rough roads.

5. In 1870, James Starley, an English inventor, created the "penny-farthing" bicycle, which had a large front wheel and a smaller rear wheel. It was named after the British coins penny and farthing because of their size difference.

6. Riding the penny-farthing was challenging and dangerous due to its high seat and the risk of falling forward.

7. In 1885, John Kemp Starley, James Starley's nephew, invented the "safety bicycle," which had two wheels of equal size and a chain-driven rear wheel. This design became the basis for modern bicycles.

8. The safety bicycle allowed for easier and safer riding, making bicycles more accessible to the general public, including women.

9. In 1888, Scottish inventor John Boyd Dunlop created the first practical pneumatic (air-filled) tire for bicycles, which provided a more comfortable ride and improved traction.

10. The introduction of pneumatic tires further popularized bicycles, as it made riding on rough roads much more tolerable.

11. In the 1890s, the "bicycle craze" swept across Europe and the United States, with millions of bicycles being manufactured and sold.

12. The bicycle's popularity led to significant social changes, such as increased mobility for women and the development of bicycle clubs and touring groups.

13. The Wright brothers, Orville and Wilbur, were bicycle manufacturers before they became famous for inventing the airplane. Their experience with bicycles influenced their aircraft designs.

14. During World War I, bicycles were used by military messengers and scouts to navigate the battlefield quickly and quietly.

15. In the 1920s, the automobile began to replace the bicycle as the primary mode of personal transportation in many countries.

16. However, the bicycle remained popular for recreation, exercise, and racing. The Tour de France, one of the most famous bicycle races, began in 1903.

17. In the 1960s and 1970s, the environmental movement and the oil crisis led to a renewed interest in bicycles as an eco-friendly and cost-effective alternative to cars.

18. The development of mountain bikes in the 1970s and 1980s expanded the range of terrain that bicycles could navigate and sparked new interest in off-road cycling.

19. Today, bicycles are used for various purposes, including transportation, recreation, exercise, and sport. They are also recognized as a sustainable and healthy mode of travel.

20. Advancements in materials, technology, and design have led to the development of increasingly specialized bicycles, such as racing bikes, BMX bikes, and electric bicycles, catering to different rider needs and preferences.

Chapter 8: The invention of the light bulb

1. In the early 1800s, inventors started experimenting with electricity to create light. They used materials like platinum and carbon to make early light bulbs.

2. Humphry Davy, an English chemist, created the first electric light in 1802 using a battery and a piece of carbon. However, it was too bright and didn't last long.

3. In 1840, Warren de la Rue, a British astronomer, created a light bulb using a coiled platinum filament. It worked well but was too expensive for practical use.

4. Joseph Swan, an English physicist, created a light bulb with a carbon filament in 1860. However, it burned out quickly and needed a better vacuum.

5. In 1879, Thomas Edison, an American inventor, created a light bulb with a carbonized bamboo filament that lasted for over 1,200 hours.

6. Edison and his team tested over 6,000 materials before finding the right one for the filament. They even tried using human hair!

7. Edison's light bulb used a glass bulb with a complete vacuum to prevent the filament from burning out too quickly.

8. In 1880, Edison opened the first electric light power station in New York City, providing electricity to 59 customers in a one-square-mile area.

9. The first widespread use of light bulbs was in New York City's financial district, where they replaced gas lamps in the early 1880s.

10. In 1881, Lewis Latimer, an African American inventor, patented a method for making carbon filaments more durable, improving the life span of light bulbs.

11. By 1904, tungsten filaments were introduced, which lasted even longer than carbon filaments and provided brighter light.

12. In 1906, the General Electric Company (GE) began selling tungsten filament light bulbs, which became the standard for many years.

13. Fluorescent light bulbs were first introduced in the 1930s. They were more energy-efficient than incandescent bulbs but contained toxic mercury.

14. In 1962, Nick Holonyak Jr., an American engineer, invented the first visible light-emitting diode (LED), which was red in color.

15. LED light bulbs became more popular in the early 2000s as they were even more energy-efficient and long-lasting than fluorescent bulbs.

16. In 2008, the European Union began phasing out incandescent light bulbs to encourage the use of more energy-efficient alternatives.

17. By 2014, several countries, including the United States, had also phased out the production and import of incandescent light bulbs.

18. Today, LED light bulbs are widely used and continue to improve in efficiency, brightness, and color options.

19. Smart light bulbs, which can be controlled by smartphones or voice assistants, have become increasingly popular in recent years.

20. The invention of the light bulb has had a profound impact on society, allowing people to work, study, and socialize even after the sun goes down.

Chapter 9: The history of the computer

1. Long ago, people used simple tools like the abacus to help them count and solve math problems. These early inventions laid the groundwork for the development of computers.

2. In the early 1800s, a mathematician named Charles Babbage designed a machine called the Analytical Engine, which could perform calculations using punch cards. Although it was never fully built, it was an important step in the history of computing.

3. During World War II, the British developed a machine called the Colossus to help them break secret German codes. It was one of the first electronic digital computers.

4. In the 1940s, a team of scientists led by John Mauchly and J. Presper Eckert built the Electronic Numerical Integrator and Computer (ENIAC), one of the first general-purpose electronic computers. It was huge, weighing 30 tons and filling an entire room.

5. Grace Hopper, a computer scientist and U.S. Navy rear admiral, invented the first compiler, a program that translates instructions written in a programming language into a form that computers can execute directly.

6. In the 1950s, computers used vacuum tubes to store and process information. These early computers were large, expensive, and generated a lot of heat.

7. The invention of the transistor in 1947 revolutionized computing. Transistors were smaller, cheaper, and more reliable than vacuum tubes, allowing computers to become more compact and efficient.

8. In 1971, the first microprocessor, the Intel 4004, was released. This tiny chip contained all the components of a computer's central processing unit (CPU) on a single integrated circuit.

9. The first personal computer, the Altair 8800, was released in 1975. It came as a kit that users had to assemble themselves and had very limited capabilities compared to modern computers.

10. Steve Jobs and Steve Wozniak, the co-founders of Apple, introduced the Apple II in 1977. It was one of the first successful mass-produced microcomputers and helped popularize personal computing.

11. In 1981, IBM introduced the IBM PC, which became the standard for personal computers in the business world. It used an operating system called MS-DOS, developed by Microsoft.

12. The first laptop computer, the Osborne 1, was released in 1981. It weighed 24 pounds and had a tiny 5-inch screen, but it paved the way for portable computing.

13. In 1984, Apple introduced the Macintosh, the first personal computer with a graphical user interface (GUI) and a mouse. This made computers more user-friendly and accessible to a wider audience.

14. The World Wide Web, invented by Tim Berners-Lee in 1989, revolutionized the way people communicate and access information. It allowed computers to connect and share data globally.

15. In the 1990s, computers became faster, cheaper, and more powerful. The introduction of CDs and DVDs allowed for the storage of large amounts of data, including music, movies, and software.

16. The first smartphones, combining the functions of a mobile phone and a computer, appeared in the early 2000s. These devices put the power of computing in people's pockets.

17. As computers became more connected, cybersecurity became increasingly important. Antivirus software and firewalls were developed to protect computers from malware and hackers.

18. Cloud computing, which allows users to store and access data and services over the internet, has become increasingly popular in recent years. This has enabled people to work and collaborate from anywhere in the world.

19. Artificial intelligence (AI) and machine learning have become increasingly important in the development of computers. These technologies allow computers to learn and make decisions based on data, without being explicitly programmed.

20. Today, computers are an essential part of our lives. They help us communicate, work, learn, and play. As technology continues to advance, the possibilities for the future of computing are endless.

Chapter 10: The creation of the steam engine

1. Long ago, people used their own strength or the power of animals to do work. But in the late 1600s, inventors began exploring ways to harness the power of steam to make machines move.

2. In 1698, Thomas Savery, an English inventor, patented the first practical steam engine. It was used to pump water out of coal mines, making it easier and safer for miners to do their jobs.

3. Thomas Newcomen, another English inventor, created an improved steam engine in 1712. It used a piston and cylinder to generate more power and was more reliable than Savery's design.

4. In 1764, James Watt, a Scottish inventor, was asked to repair a Newcomen engine. He noticed that it wasted a lot of energy and set out to make it more efficient.

5. Watt's improved steam engine, patented in 1769, used a separate condenser to cool the steam, which greatly increased its efficiency and power output. This design became the basis for many later steam engines.

6. The steam engine revolutionized transportation. In 1802, Richard Trevithick, an English engineer, built the first steam-powered locomotive. It paved the way for the development of steam-powered trains.

7. Robert Fulton, an American inventor, built the first successful steamboat in 1807. Named the Clermont, it carried passengers up and down the Hudson River in New York.

8. George Stephenson, known as the "Father of Railways," built the first public inter-city railway line in the world to use steam locomotives. The Stockton and Darlington Railway opened in England in 1825.

9. The steam engine also transformed manufacturing. It provided a reliable and powerful source of energy for factories, allowing them to produce goods on a much larger scale than before.

10. The Industrial Revolution, which began in the late 1700s, was largely driven by the steam engine. It led to the growth of cities, the rise of factories, and major changes in the way people lived and worked.

11. The steam engine also had a significant impact on agriculture. Steam-powered machines like tractors and threshers made it possible to farm larger areas of land more efficiently.

12. Steam power played a crucial role in the expansion of European colonialism in the 19th century. Steam-powered ships and trains made it easier for European nations to transport goods, people, and military forces around the world.

13. The steam engine also drove the development of new technologies. For example, the steam turbine, invented by Sir Charles Parsons in 1884, became an important source of power for generating electricity.

14. The steam engine's influence extended beyond technology. It inspired art, literature, and music, with many artists and writers celebrating the power and potential of steam in their works.

15. However, the steam engine also had negative impacts. The burning of coal to power steam engines contributed to air pollution and health problems in cities.

16. The rise of steam power also led to social and economic changes that were not always positive. Many skilled craftsmen lost their jobs as factories replaced small workshops, and working conditions in some factories were harsh and dangerous.

17. Despite these challenges, the steam engine's influence continued well into the 20th century. Steam turbines, for example, remained an important source of power for ships and power plants until the rise of diesel engines and other alternatives.

18. Today, the steam engine is no longer the dominant source of power it once was. However, its legacy lives on in the many technologies and industries it helped to create.

19. Some organizations and enthusiasts still preserve and operate steam engines as a way to celebrate their historical significance and engineering achievements. Many museums feature exhibits on the history and impact of steam power.

20. The story of the steam engine is a testament to human ingenuity and the power of invention to transform the world. It reminds us that even the most complex challenges can be overcome with creativity, perseverance, and a willingness to imagine new possibilities.

Chapter 11: The invention of the camera

1. Long ago, people could only capture images by painting or drawing them. But in the early 1800s, inventors began experimenting with ways to capture images using light and chemistry.

2. The first successful photograph was taken in 1826 by Joseph Nicéphore Niépce, a French inventor. He used a camera obscura and a pewter plate coated with a light-sensitive material to capture an image of his courtyard. The exposure took eight hours!

3. In 1839, Louis Daguerre, another French inventor, introduced the daguerreotype, the first commercially successful photographic process. It used a polished silver-plated copper sheet to capture images with incredible detail.

4. The same year, Henry Fox Talbot, an English scientist, invented the calotype process, which used paper coated with silver chloride to create negative images that could be used to make multiple positive prints.

5. In 1888, George Eastman, an American inventor and businessman, introduced the Kodak camera. It used roll film and came pre-loaded with enough film for 100 exposures, making photography accessible to the masses.

6. The first color photograph was taken in 1861 by James Clerk Maxwell, a Scottish scientist. He used three different filters (red, green, and blue) to capture separate images that were then combined to create a full-color photograph.

7. In 1900, the Brownie camera, an inexpensive and easy-to-use camera, was introduced by Eastman Kodak. It helped to democratize photography and make it a popular hobby for people around the world.

8. The first 35mm camera, the Leica, was introduced in 1925 by Ernst Leitz, a German optical engineer. It used a compact design and high-quality lenses to produce sharp, detailed images.

9. In 1948, Edwin Land, an American inventor and co-founder of the Polaroid Corporation, introduced the first instant camera. It used a special film that developed and printed photographs within minutes.

10. The first digital camera was invented in 1975 by Steven Sasson, an engineer at Eastman Kodak. It used a CCD (charge-coupled device) sensor to capture images and store them on a cassette tape.

11. In 1994, the first commercially available digital camera, the Apple QuickTake, was introduced. It could store up to eight images at a resolution of 640x480 pixels.

12. The invention of the camera changed the way people saw the world. It allowed them to capture and preserve moments in time, from important historical events to everyday scenes of life.

13. Cameras played a crucial role in the development of modern journalism, allowing reporters to document news and events with powerful visual evidence.

14. Photography also became an important tool for scientists, allowing them to capture images of things too small, too fast, or too distant for the human eye to see.

15. The rise of photography as an art form in the late 19th and early 20th centuries led to new ways of seeing and representing the world. Photographers like Alfred Stieglitz and Ansel Adams elevated photography to the level of fine art.

16. The development of motion picture cameras in the late 19th century paved the way for the birth of the film industry, which would go on to become one of the most influential forms of media in the 20th century.

17. The introduction of lightweight, portable cameras in the mid-20th century allowed people to document their own lives and experiences like never before, creating a vast visual record of everyday life.

18. The rise of digital photography in the late 20th and early 21st centuries revolutionized the way people capture, store, and share images. With the advent of smartphones, almost everyone now has a camera in their pocket.

19. Despite the many advances in camera technology over the years, the basic principles of photography - using light to capture images on a light-sensitive surface - have remained the same since the early days of the medium.

20. Today, cameras continue to evolve and shape the way we see and remember the world around us. From high-resolution digital cameras to 360-degree video cameras, the possibilities for capturing and sharing images are endless.

Chapter 12: The development of the automobile

1. Long ago, people traveled by foot, on horseback, or in horse-drawn carriages. But in the late 1800s, inventors began experimenting with new ways to power vehicles using engines.

2. One of the earliest attempts at creating a self-propelled vehicle was the "Fardier à vapeur," built by French inventor Nicolas-Joseph Cugnot in 1769. It was a steam-powered tricycle that could carry up to four passengers.

3. In 1886, German inventor Karl Benz patented the Benz Patent-Motorwagen, widely regarded as the first modern automobile. It had three wheels and a gasoline-powered engine.

4. That same year, Gottlieb Daimler and Wilhelm Maybach, also German inventors, created a four-wheeled vehicle powered by a gasoline engine. It was the first automobile to have four wheels.

5. In 1893, Charles and Frank Duryea, American brothers, built the first successful gasoline-powered car in the United States. They founded the Duryea Motor Wagon Company, the first American automobile manufacturing company.

6. In 1908, Henry Ford introduced the Model T, the first automobile to be mass-produced on an assembly line. This made cars more affordable and accessible to the general public.

7. The assembly line revolutionized manufacturing and became a symbol of the Industrial Age. It allowed factories to produce cars more quickly and efficiently, which helped to drive down prices.

8. As more people began to own cars, there was a growing need for better roads. In the early 1900s, the United States government began funding the construction of a national highway system.

9. The rise of the automobile also led to the growth of new industries, such as oil and rubber production, as well as the development of new technologies like traffic lights and parking meters.

10. In the 1920s, cars became a symbol of freedom and mobility for many Americans. People could now travel longer distances more easily, which opened up new opportunities for work and leisure.

11. During World War II, many automobile factories were converted to produce military vehicles and equipment. After the war, these factories returned to producing cars for the growing consumer market.

12. In the 1950s and 60s, cars became an important part of American culture. Drive-in movie theaters and restaurants became popular, and owning a car became a symbol of prosperity and independence.

13. However, the growth of the automobile industry also had negative consequences. Traffic congestion and air pollution became major problems in many cities, and car accidents became a leading cause of death and injury.

14. In response to these challenges, governments began to regulate the automobile industry more closely. Safety features like seat belts and airbags became mandatory, and emissions standards were introduced to reduce air pollution.

15. In the 1970s, rising gas prices and concerns about foreign oil dependence led to a renewed interest in fuel-efficient and alternative-fuel vehicles. The first modern electric cars were introduced during this time.

16. In the 1980s and 90s, computerization and automation began to transform the automobile industry. Cars became more technologically advanced, with features like electronic fuel injection and antilock brakes.

17. The late 20th and early 21st centuries saw a growing awareness of the environmental impact of automobiles. Hybrid and electric vehicles became more popular as people looked for ways to reduce their carbon footprint.

18. Today, self-driving cars are one of the most exciting frontiers in automobile technology. Companies like Tesla, Google, and Uber are investing heavily in the development of autonomous vehicles.

19. Despite these advances, the basic principle of the automobile has remained the same since the days of Karl Benz and Gottlieb Daimler: a vehicle powered by an engine that can transport people and goods from one place to another.

20. The story of the automobile is a testament to human ingenuity and the power of technology to transform society. From the earliest steam-powered carriages to the latest electric and self-driving cars, the automobile has played a central role in shaping the modern world.

Chapter 13: The story behind the first robot

1. The word "robot" comes from the Czech word "robota," which means "forced labor." It was first used in a 1920 play called "R.U.R." (Rossum's Universal Robots) by Czech writer Karel Čapek.

2. In 1928, one of the first humanoid robots, named Eric, was exhibited at the Model Engineers Society in London. It was made of aluminum and could move its arms, head, and eyes, and even speak a few words.

3. In the 1940s, American inventor George Devol created the first programmable robot, known as the "Unimate." It was used in a General Motors factory to help with assembly line tasks.

4. The first electronic autonomous robots were created by American scientist William Grey Walter in the late 1940s. Named Elmer and Elsie, these robots could navigate their environment and avoid obstacles using light sensors.

5. In 1954, George Devol and Joseph Engelberger founded the world's first robot company, Unimation. They developed the first industrial robot, the Unimate, which was used in a GM plant to handle hot metal parts.

6. In the 1960s, researchers at the Stanford Research Institute created "Shakey," a mobile robot that could navigate its environment using a camera, range finder, and onboard computer. It was one of the first robots to use artificial intelligence.

7. The first walking humanoid robot, "WABOT-1," was developed in Japan in 1973. It could walk, communicate in Japanese, and even measure distances and directions using external receptors.

8. In the late 1970s, the "Stanford Cart," a robot developed at Stanford University, successfully navigated a room full of obstacles using a camera and onboard computer. This demonstrated the potential for robots to navigate complex environments.

9. The first "pick and place" robot, the "Silver Arm," was developed in 1974 at the University of Edinburgh. It used touch and pressure sensors to manipulate objects, paving the way for more advanced industrial robots.

10. In 1986, Honda began developing humanoid robots, leading to the creation of the "P-series" robots. These robots could walk, climb stairs, and even respond to simple voice commands.

11. The "Genghis" robot, developed at MIT in the late 1980s, was one of the first autonomous robots to use a behavior-based control system. This allowed it to navigate its environment and perform tasks without explicit programming.

12. In the 1990s, NASA began using robots to explore Mars. The "Sojourner" rover, part of the Mars Pathfinder mission, demonstrated the potential for robots to explore other planets.

13. The "Furby," a toy robot released in 1998, was one of the first mass-produced robots for home use. It could speak, learn, and interact with its environment using sensors and a simple computer.

14. In the early 2000s, the U.S. military began using robots for battlefield operations. The "PackBot," developed by iRobot, was used to search caves in Afghanistan and dispose of explosives in Iraq.

15. The "Roomba," released by iRobot in 2002, was one of the first successful home cleaning robots. It used sensors to navigate and clean floors automatically, paving the way for more advanced home robots.

16. In 2004, the "Spirit" and "Opportunity" rovers landed on Mars, beginning a new era of planetary exploration. These robots used advanced sensors and onboard computers to search for evidence of water and past life on Mars.

17. The "BigDog," developed by Boston Dynamics in the mid-2000s, was a four-legged robot designed to navigate rough terrain. It used sensors and a computer to maintain balance and could even recover from being kicked or pushed.

18. The "Nao," a humanoid robot developed by Aldebaran Robotics, was released in 2008. It was designed for education and research and could be programmed to walk, talk, and even recognize faces and objects.

19. In 2011, IBM's "Watson" computer competed on the TV show Jeopardy! against human champions, showcasing the potential for artificial intelligence and natural language processing in robotics.

20. Today, robots are used in a wide variety of fields, from manufacturing and medicine to space exploration and home assistance. As technology continues to advance, the possibilities for robots to help and interact with humans in new and exciting ways are endless.

Chapter 14: The invention of the microscope

1. The first microscopes were invented in the late 16th century by Dutch spectacle makers Zacharias Janssen and his father Hans. They discovered that by putting two lenses together, they could make objects appear much larger than they really were.

2. In 1665, English scientist Robert Hooke used a microscope to examine a thin slice of cork. He discovered that it was made up of tiny boxes, which he called "cells" because they reminded him of the cells that monks lived in.

3. Dutch scientist Antonie van Leeuwenhoek, also known as the "Father of Microbiology," made significant improvements to the microscope in the late 17th century. He used them to observe bacteria, yeast, and even blood cells for the first time.

4. Leeuwenhoek's microscopes were very simple, using only a single lens. However, he was able to make lenses of such high quality that he could magnify objects up to 300 times their original size.

5. In 1674, Leeuwenhoek discovered microorganisms in a drop of water. He called them "animalcules," which means "tiny animals." This discovery led to a whole new field of study known as microbiology.

6. The compound microscope, which uses two or more lenses to magnify objects, was invented in the early 17th century. However, it wasn't until the 19th century that significant improvements were made to the design.

7. In 1830, British scientist Joseph Jackson Lister discovered that by combining lenses in a certain way, he could reduce the distortion and color fringing that had plagued earlier microscopes. This made it possible to see objects more clearly and in greater detail.

8. German physicist Ernst Abbe made further improvements to the microscope in the late 19th century. He developed a mathematical formula that allowed for the creation of high-quality lenses with less distortion.

9. In 1931, German physicist Ernst Ruska and electrical engineer Max Knoll invented the electron microscope. This type of microscope uses a beam of electrons instead of light to magnify

objects, allowing for much higher magnification than traditional microscopes.

10. The invention of the microscope revolutionized the field of biology. It allowed scientists to observe and study the tiniest living organisms and structures, leading to a better understanding of how life works at the most basic level.

11. Microscopes have also been used to make important discoveries in fields like medicine and materials science. For example, the invention of the microscope led to the development of the germ theory of disease, which states that many diseases are caused by microorganisms.

12. Today, there are many different types of microscopes, each with its own strengths and weaknesses. Some are designed to observe living cells, while others are used to study the structure of materials at the atomic level.

13. One type of microscope, called a scanning tunneling microscope, can even be used to move individual atoms around. This has led to the development of new fields like nanotechnology, which involves manipulating matter at the atomic and molecular scale.

14. Despite all the advances in microscope technology, some of the most important discoveries in science were made using very simple microscopes. For example, in 1677 Antonie van Leeuwenhoek discovered sperm cells using a single-lens microscope that he made himself.

15. The invention of the microscope has also had an impact on art and popular culture. Many artists have used microscopic images as inspiration for their work, while movies and TV shows often feature scenes where characters use microscopes to make important discoveries.

16. Microscopes can be used to observe a wide variety of specimens, from tiny bacteria and viruses to crystals, fibers, and even computer chips. Each type of specimen requires a different type of preparation and observation technique.

17. One of the most exciting applications of microscopy is in the field of regenerative medicine. By studying how cells and tissues grow and develop under the microscope, scientists hope to find new ways to treat diseases and injuries by regenerating damaged or lost body parts.

18. The invention of the microscope has also led to the development of new technologies like microfluidics, which involves manipulating tiny amounts of fluids using microscopic channels and valves. This has applications in fields like drug discovery and disease diagnosis.

19. Microscopes have even been sent into space to study how plants and animals respond to microgravity. In 2018, a microscope was sent to the International Space Station to observe how the structure of materials changes in space.

20. The story of the microscope is a testament to human curiosity and ingenuity. From the first simple lenses made by Dutch spectacle makers to the cutting-edge electron microscopes of today, the invention of the microscope has opened up a whole new world of discovery and understanding.

Chapter 15: The creation of the refrigerator

1. Long ago, people used natural methods to keep their food cool, such as storing it underground or using ice from frozen lakes and rivers. But in the mid-1800s, inventors began experimenting with artificial cooling methods.

2. In 1805, an American inventor named Oliver Evans designed the first refrigeration machine. It used vapor to cool water, but it was never built.

3. In 1834, an American inventor named Jacob Perkins built the first practical refrigeration machine. It used ether to cool water, but it was not very efficient and was never widely used.

4. In 1844, an American physician named John Gorrie built a machine that used compressed air to make ice. He hoped to use it to cool hospital rooms and treat patients with fever, but his idea never caught on.

5. In the late 1800s, a German engineer named Carl von Linde developed a more efficient refrigeration machine that used ammonia as the cooling agent. His invention was used to cool beer and other drinks.

6. In 1876, a French monk named Marcel Audiffren invented a small, portable refrigeration machine that used sulfuric acid and water to cool air. It was used to cool drinks and make ice cream.

7. In 1894, an American inventor named Nathaniel Wales developed a refrigeration machine that used compressed ammonia to cool air. It was more efficient than earlier designs and was used to cool meat and other perishable foods.

8. In 1913, an American inventor named Fred Wolf invented the first electric refrigerator for home use. It used a compressor to cool air and had a separate freezer compartment.

9. In 1923, an American company called Frigidaire introduced the first self-contained electric refrigerator. It had a compressor, condenser, and evaporator all in one unit, making it easier to manufacture and install.

10. By the 1930s, electric refrigerators had become common in American homes. They revolutionized the way people stored and prepared food, allowing them to keep perishable items fresh for much longer.

11. During World War II, refrigeration technology was used to preserve blood and medicine for wounded soldiers. After the war, new advances in refrigeration led to the development of frozen foods and ice cream.

12. In the 1950s, refrigerators became more colorful and stylish, with new features like automatic defrosting and adjustable shelves. Some even had built-in radios or televisions.

13. In the 1960s and 70s, new environmental concerns led to the development of more energy-efficient refrigerators. These used less electricity and produced fewer harmful emissions.

14. In the 1980s and 90s, refrigerators became more computerized, with digital controls and sensors that could automatically adjust the temperature and humidity levels.

15. Today, refrigerators come in all shapes and sizes, from small dorm-room models to large, high-tech units with built-in cameras and touch screens. Some even have Wi-Fi connectivity and can be controlled from a smartphone.

16. The invention of the refrigerator has had a huge impact on modern life. It has made it possible to store and transport food over long distances, reducing waste and improving nutrition.

17. Refrigeration technology has also played a key role in the development of modern medicine, allowing hospitals to store vaccines, medicines, and other perishable supplies.

18. In developing countries, access to refrigeration is still limited, leading to high levels of food waste and spoilage. Organizations like the World Health Organization are working to bring refrigeration technology to these areas.

19. In the future, new advances in refrigeration technology could lead to even more efficient and environmentally-friendly refrigerators. Some researchers are even exploring the use of magnetic cooling, which uses magnets to cool air without any moving parts.

20. The story of the refrigerator is a testament to the power of human ingenuity and the impact that a single invention can have on the world. From the early experiments of Oliver Evans and Jacob Perkins to the high-tech models of today, the refrigerator has transformed the way we live and eat, making our lives easier and healthier.

Chapter 16: The invention of the calculator

1. Long ago, people used simple tools like the abacus to do math. But as math problems became more complex, inventors started looking for better ways to calculate.

2. In the early 1600s, a Scottish mathematician named John Napier invented a tool called "Napier's bones." It used a set of numbered rods to help with multiplication and division.

3. In 1623, a German astronomer named Wilhelm Schickard designed a mechanical calculator that could add and subtract. Sadly, the original machine was destroyed in a fire.

4. In 1820, a French mathematician named Charles Xavier Thomas de Colmar created the first commercially produced mechanical calculator. It could perform all four basic math functions.

5. In the late 1800s, a Swedish engineer named Willgodt Odhner invented a pin-wheel calculator that became very popular. It was smaller and cheaper than earlier mechanical calculators.

6. During World War II, the U.S. military needed a fast and accurate way to calculate artillery firing tables. A team of mathematicians and engineers created the Electronic Numerical Integrator and Computer (ENIAC) to do the job.

7. In 1948, a Japanese company called Casio released the first electric calculator. It used relay circuits to perform calculations.

8. In 1961, the British company Bell Punch released the "Sumlock ANITA," the world's first all-electronic desktop calculator. It used vacuum tubes and weighed nearly 60 pounds!

9. In 1963, an Italian company called Olivetti introduced the "Programma 101," the first commercial programmable desktop computer. It could be used for complex math and even some simple programming.

10. In the early 1970s, calculators became smaller and more affordable thanks to the invention of the microprocessor. Companies like Texas Instruments and Hewlett-Packard started selling handheld calculators.

11. In 1972, Hewlett-Packard released the HP-35, the first scientific calculator. It could perform trigonometric and exponential functions, making it popular with engineers and scientists.

12. In 1974, Texas Instruments released the SR-50, the first handheld calculator with a single-chip microprocessor. It was smaller and cheaper than earlier calculators.

13. In 1985, Casio released the FX-7000G, the world's first graphing calculator. It could plot graphs and solve equations, making it a powerful tool for math students.

14. In the 1990s, calculators began to incorporate more advanced features like spreadsheets, databases, and even basic computer algebra systems. Some models could connect to computers and share data.

15. Today, most calculators are digital and can perform a wide range of functions. Some are even built into smartphones and computers.

16. Despite the rise of computers and smartphones, dedicated calculators are still widely used in schools and offices around the world. They are often required for math exams and standardized tests.

17. In addition to basic calculators, there are now many specialized calculators for fields like finance, engineering, and programming. These calculators can perform complex calculations and simulations.

18. Some high-end calculators even have full-color screens and can run advanced graphing and geometry software. They are like miniature computers designed specifically for math.

19. The invention of the calculator has had a huge impact on the way we do math. It has made complex calculations faster and more accurate, and has opened up new possibilities for fields like science and engineering.

20. As technology continues to advance, it's likely that calculators will become even more powerful and versatile. But no matter how advanced they become, they will always be an important tool for anyone who needs to do math quickly and accurately.

Chapter 17: The development of the compass

1. Long ago, people used the sun and stars to navigate. But what happened when the sky was cloudy or dark? Around 2,000 years ago, the Chinese discovered a solution: the magnetic compass.

2. The first compasses were made from lodestones, naturally magnetized pieces of iron ore. When suspended freely, lodestones always pointed in a north-south direction.

3. The Chinese began using lodestones for navigation as early as the 11th century. They shaped the stones into spoons and placed them on bronze plates to create early compasses.

4. In the 12th century, Chinese sailors improved the compass by mounting the lodestone on a pivot, allowing it to rotate freely. This made it easier to read and more accurate.

5. The compass spread to Europe in the 13th century, where it quickly became an essential tool for navigation. European sailors used compasses to explore the world and establish new trade routes.

6. In the 14th century, Italian inventor Flavio Gioja made an important improvement to the compass. He added a compass card, a rotating dial marked with cardinal directions, making the compass easier to read.

7. The compass played a crucial role in the Age of Exploration in the 15th and 16th centuries. Explorers like Christopher Columbus and Vasco da Gama used compasses to navigate across vast oceans and discover new lands.

8. In the 18th century, Swedish scientist Carl Linnaeus discovered that some animals, like birds and sea turtles, had a natural compass in their brains. This allowed them to navigate long distances without getting lost.

9. In the 19th century, British physicist William Thomson (also known as Lord Kelvin) invented the modern compass. It used a lightweight magnet and a dampening fluid to make the needle more stable and accurate.

10. During World War I and II, the military used compasses extensively for land and sea navigation. Specialized compasses were developed for use in tanks, ships, and aircraft.

11. In the 1920s, American inventor Clarence Birdseye developed a wristwatch compass for use by soldiers and explorers. It was small, lightweight, and could be worn on the wrist for easy access.

12. The invention of the gyrocompass in the early 20th century provided an alternative to the magnetic compass. Gyrocompasses use the Earth's rotation to find true north, making them more accurate than magnetic compasses.

13. In the 1960s, the U.S. Navy developed the first satellite navigation system, called TRANSIT. It used a network of satellites to provide accurate location and direction information to ships and submarines.

14. The Global Positioning System (GPS), developed by the U.S. military in the 1970s, revolutionized navigation. GPS uses a network of satellites to provide precise location and direction information to receivers on Earth.

15. Today, most smartphones have built-in GPS and digital compasses, making navigation easier than ever. However, knowing how to use a traditional compass is still an important skill for outdoor enthusiasts and adventurers.

16. Compasses are used in many different fields beyond navigation. Geologists use compasses to measure the orientation of rock formations, while archaeologists use them to map out excavation sites.

17. In the sport of orienteering, competitors use a map and compass to navigate through unfamiliar terrain to specific checkpoints. The fastest person to reach all the checkpoints wins.

18. Some animals, like honeybees and homing pigeons, use the Earth's magnetic field to navigate. Scientists are still studying how they are able to detect and use this invisible force.

19. The compass rose, a symbol found on maps and charts, is named after the compass. It shows the cardinal and intermediate directions and is used to orient the map with the real world.

20. The invention of the compass changed the course of human history. It allowed people to explore new lands, establish trade routes, and expand their knowledge of the world. Today, the compass remains an essential tool for anyone who needs to find their way.

Chapter 18: The story behind the first hot air balloon

1. Long ago, people dreamed of flying like birds. They watched the clouds and imagined floating high above the ground. But it wasn't until 1783 that the first humans took to the skies in a hot air balloon.

2. The inventors of the hot air balloon were two French brothers named Joseph-Michel and Jacques-Étienne Montgolfier. They came from a family of paper manufacturers and were fascinated by the idea of flight.

3. The Montgolfier brothers noticed that smoke always rose upward. They thought that if they could capture this rising smoke in a bag, it might lift the bag into the air.

4. In 1782, the brothers began experimenting with small paper bags filled with hot air. They discovered that the bags would rise to the ceiling and float there until the air cooled.

5. Encouraged by their success, the Montgolfiers built larger and larger paper bags. They filled them with hot air by burning straw and wood beneath an opening at the bottom of the bag.

6. On June 4, 1783, the Montgolfiers gave their first public demonstration of a hot air balloon in their hometown of Annonay, France. The balloon rose to a height of 6,000 feet and traveled over a mile before landing safely.

7. News of the Montgolfiers' invention spread quickly throughout France. King Louis XVI and Queen Marie Antoinette were so impressed that they invited the brothers to Paris for a demonstration.

8. On September 19, 1783, the Montgolfiers launched a hot air balloon from the Palace of Versailles in front of a huge crowd. This time, the balloon carried three passengers: a sheep, a duck, and a rooster.

9. The animals landed safely after an eight-minute flight, proving that living creatures could survive the trip. The stage was set for the first human flight.

10. On November 21, 1783, French aristocrat Pilâtre de Rozier and army officer François Laurent d'Arlandes became the first humans to fly in a hot air balloon. They flew for 25 minutes over Paris, reaching a height of 3,000 feet.

11. The Montgolfier brothers continued to improve their balloon design, using stronger and more durable materials like linen and silk. They also experimented with different shapes and sizes.

12. In 1785, French balloonist Jean-Pierre Blanchard and American doctor John Jeffries became the first to cross the English Channel by hot air balloon. The trip took about 2.5 hours.

13. Hot air balloons became a popular attraction at fairs and exhibitions throughout Europe and America. People marveled at the sight of these giant, colorful balloons floating through the sky.

14. During the American Civil War, the Union Army used hot air balloons for reconnaissance and spying on Confederate troops. The balloons were tethered to the ground by ropes and could carry observers high above the battlefield.

15. In 1932, Swiss scientist Auguste Piccard became the first person to reach the stratosphere in a hot air balloon. He reached a height of over 52,000 feet, setting a new altitude record.

16. During World War II, the Japanese military launched thousands of hydrogen-filled "fire balloons" across the Pacific Ocean, hoping to start forest fires in the western United States. Most of the balloons failed to reach their target.

17. In the 1960s, hot air ballooning experienced a resurgence in popularity. New materials like nylon and propane burners made it easier and safer to fly balloons.

18. In 1987, British entrepreneur Richard Branson and Swedish aeronaut Per Lindstrand became the first to cross the Atlantic Ocean in a hot air balloon. The trip took about 31 hours.

19. Today, hot air balloons are used for recreation, advertising, and scientific research. Some balloons are designed to look like animals, cartoon characters, or famous landmarks.

20. The invention of the hot air balloon marked the beginning of human flight. It showed that with imagination and perseverance, people could achieve what seemed impossible. Today, the sight of a hot air balloon floating peacefully through the sky still inspires wonder and delight.

Chapter 19: The invention of the sewing machine

1. Long ago, people made clothes by sewing them by hand. It was a slow and tedious process that took a lot of time and effort. But in the early 1800s, inventors began to look for ways to make sewing easier and faster.

2. One of the first attempts at a sewing machine was made by an Englishman named Thomas Saint in 1790. He created a design for a machine that could sew leather and canvas using a needle and thread.

3. In 1830, a French tailor named Barthélemy Thimonnier patented a sewing machine that used a hooked needle and a foot pedal to create a chain stitch. However, other tailors who feared losing their jobs burned down his factory.

4. An American inventor named Walter Hunt created a sewing machine in 1834 that used an eye-pointed needle and two spools of thread to create a lockstitch. However, he abandoned the project and didn't patent his invention.

5. In 1844, an Englishman named John Fisher invented a sewing machine that used a horizontal needle and a vertical needle to create a locking stitch. However, his machine was never commercially produced.

6. The first practical and commercially successful sewing machine was invented by Elias Howe in 1845. His machine used a curved needle with an eye at the point and a shuttle to create a lockstitch.

7. However, Howe had trouble finding investors for his invention and ended up selling the patent rights to his brother. He later had to fight in court to reclaim his rights and receive royalties for his invention.

8. In 1851, Isaac Singer invented a sewing machine that used a vertical needle and a foot pedal. His machine was easier to use and more efficient than earlier models, and it quickly became popular.

9. Singer's sewing machine was the first to be mass-produced and sold to the public. He used innovative marketing techniques, like installment plans and trade-ins, to make his machines more affordable and accessible.

10. The sewing machine revolutionized the clothing industry and made it possible to produce clothes much faster and more efficiently than ever before. It also led to the creation of new types of clothes, like ready-to-wear garments.

11. In the late 1800s, sewing machines became smaller, lighter, and more portable. This made it possible for people to sew at home and start their own small businesses.

12. The sewing machine also played a role in the women's rights movement. It gave women the ability to earn their own income and become more independent.

13. During the American Civil War, sewing machines were used to make uniforms and other clothing for soldiers. They helped to keep the troops clothed and equipped throughout the long and bloody conflict.

14. In the early 1900s, electric sewing machines were introduced. They were faster and more powerful than earlier models and made it possible to sew through thicker fabrics like denim and leather.

15. During World War II, sewing machines were used to make parachutes, tents, and other military equipment. They played a crucial role in the war effort and helped to keep soldiers safe and comfortable.

16. In the 1950s and 60s, sewing machines became more affordable and easier to use. Many households had their own sewing machines, and sewing became a popular hobby and creative outlet.

17. Today, sewing machines are used in a wide range of industries, from fashion and home decor to automotive and aerospace. They are an essential tool for anyone who works with fabric or textiles.

18. Modern sewing machines are highly computerized and can perform a wide range of functions, from embroidery and quilting to buttonholes and zippers. They are faster, more precise, and more versatile than ever before.

19. Despite the many advances in technology, the basic principles of the sewing machine have remained the same since the days of Elias Howe and Isaac Singer. It is a testament to the ingenuity and creativity of these early inventors.

20. The invention of the sewing machine changed the world in countless ways. It made clothing more affordable and accessible, created new industries and jobs, and gave people the power to express themselves through fashion and design. It is a true icon of the modern age.

Chapter 20: The creation of the telescope

1. Long ago, people looked up at the night sky and wondered about the stars and planets. They could only see what their eyes allowed them to see. But then, in the early 1600s, a new invention changed everything: the telescope.

2. The first telescope was invented by a Dutch eyeglass maker named Hans Lippershey in 1608. He discovered that by putting two lenses together in a tube, he could make distant objects appear closer and larger.

3. News of Lippershey's invention spread quickly throughout Europe. Many people were excited by the idea of being able to see things that were far away, like ships on the horizon or birds in the sky.

4. One person who was particularly interested in the telescope was an Italian scientist named Galileo Galilei. He heard about the invention and decided to build his own version.

5. Galileo's telescope was much more powerful than Lippershey's. It could magnify objects up to 30 times their original size. When Galileo pointed his telescope at the night sky, he was amazed by what he saw.

6. Through his telescope, Galileo discovered that the moon had mountains and valleys, just like Earth. He also saw that Jupiter had four moons orbiting around it, which helped to prove that not everything revolved around the Earth.

7. Galileo's discoveries with the telescope challenged many of the accepted ideas about the universe at the time. Some people were excited by his findings, while others were threatened by them.

8. In England, a mathematician named Thomas Harriot also built his own telescope and used it to study the moon. He made detailed drawings of the lunar surface, which were some of the first ever made.

9. As telescopes became more powerful, astronomers were able to see even more of the universe. In 1781, William Herschel discovered the planet Uranus using a telescope he built himself.

10. In the 1800s, telescopes became larger and more sophisticated. The Leviathan of Parsonstown, built by the Earl of Rosse in Ireland, had a mirror that was 6 feet in diameter and could gather more light than any other telescope at the time.

11. In the early 1900s, the Hooker Telescope at the Mount Wilson Observatory in California became the largest telescope in the world. It had a mirror that was 100 inches in diameter and was used to study distant galaxies and nebulae.

12. In 1990, the Hubble Space Telescope was launched into orbit around the Earth. It provided astronomers with stunning images of the universe, including distant galaxies, stellar nurseries, and even planets in our own solar system.

13. Today, telescopes come in many different shapes and sizes. Some are small enough to fit in your pocket, while others are as big as a house. Some telescopes are even located in space, like the James Webb Space Telescope.

14. Telescopes have also been used for purposes beyond astronomy. During the American Civil War, both the Union and Confederate armies used telescopes to spy on each other's movements.

15. In the 1960s, the United States used telescopes to take photographs of Soviet military bases from space. These images helped to provide valuable intelligence during the Cold War.

16. Telescopes have also been used to study the Earth itself. Scientists have used telescopes to monitor changes in the Earth's climate, track the movement of wildlife, and even search for natural resources.

17. In the future, telescopes may help us to answer some of the biggest questions about the universe, like whether there is life on other planets or what happened during the Big Bang.

18. One of the most exciting prospects for future telescopes is the ability to study exoplanets, or planets that orbit around other stars. Scientists hope to use telescopes to search for signs of life on these distant worlds.

19. Despite all the advances in telescope technology over the years, one thing has remained constant: the sense of wonder and curiosity that they inspire in people of all ages.

20. The invention of the telescope opened up a whole new world for humanity. It allowed us to see things that were once invisible and to explore the vastness of the universe. It is a testament to the power of human ingenuity and the endless possibilities of scientific discovery.

Chapter 21: The invention of the microwave oven

1. Did you know that the microwave oven was invented by accident? It all started during World War II when a scientist named Percy Spencer was working on radar technology.

2. One day, while Spencer was standing in front of a magnetron, a device that generates microwaves, he noticed that the candy bar in his pocket had melted. This gave him an idea.

3. Spencer experimented with different foods, including popcorn kernels, which popped when exposed to microwaves. He realized that microwaves could cook food quickly and efficiently.

4. In 1945, Spencer and his employer, Raytheon, filed a patent for the first microwave oven. It was called the "Radarange" and was about the size of a refrigerator.

5. The first microwave ovens were too large and expensive for home use. They were mainly used in restaurants and on ships to reheat food quickly.

6. In 1967, the first countertop microwave oven was introduced by Amana, a subsidiary of Raytheon. It was called the "Radarange" and cost about $500, which was equivalent to about $3,500 today.

7. Despite the high cost, microwave ovens became increasingly popular in the 1970s and 1980s. Prices dropped as more companies began manufacturing them, and they became a staple in many homes.

8. Microwave ovens work by using microwaves to heat up the water molecules in food. This causes the food to heat up quickly and evenly, without the need for a flame or heating element.

9. One of the first foods to be cooked in a microwave oven was popcorn. In 1981, Orville Redenbacher introduced the first microwave popcorn, which became an instant hit.

10. Microwave ovens have come a long way since their invention. Today, they come in a variety of sizes and styles, with features like sensor cooking, programmable settings, and even built-in grills.

11. Microwave ovens have also been used for purposes beyond cooking food. In the 1980s, some people used them to dry wet books and documents, as the microwaves could quickly evaporate the moisture.

12. In the 1990s, a company called Microwave Energy Applications developed a microwave oven that could sterilize medical equipment. This helped to reduce the risk of infection in hospitals and clinics.

13. Microwave ovens have also been used in scientific research. In 2003, a team of scientists used a microwave oven to create a new type of material called "metal organic frameworks," which have potential applications in hydrogen storage and carbon capture.

14. In 2008, a study found that microwaving tea could actually improve its antioxidant properties. The researchers found that microwaving green tea for one minute could increase its antioxidant activity by up to 20%.

15. Despite their many benefits, microwave ovens have also been the subject of some misconceptions. One common myth is that microwaving food can make it radioactive or unsafe to eat, but this is not true.

16. Another myth is that microwaves can leak radiation and cause harm to people nearby. While it is true that microwaves can leak from a damaged or faulty oven, the amount of radiation is usually very low and not harmful to humans.

17. Microwave ovens have also been used in some unusual ways. In the 1980s, a Canadian man named Dave Dunlop used a microwave oven to create a "microwave birdhouse" that could keep birds warm in the winter.

18. In 2006, a group of MIT students used a microwave oven to create a "microwave drill" that could drill through concrete. The drill used microwaves to melt and vaporize the concrete, creating a hole.

19. Today, microwave ovens are an essential appliance in many homes and workplaces around the world. They have revolutionized the way we cook and reheat food, saving time and energy in the process.

20. The invention of the microwave oven is a testament to the power of curiosity and serendipity. Who would have thought that a melted candy bar could lead to a device that has changed the way we live and eat? It just goes to show that sometimes the greatest inventions come from the most unexpected places.

Chapter 22: The development of the electric motor

1. The electric motor is a device that converts electrical energy into mechanical energy. It has revolutionized the way we live and work, powering everything from tiny toys to huge machines.

2. The first electric motor was invented by Michael Faraday in 1821. He discovered that when an electric current passed through a wire near a magnet, the wire would rotate around the magnet.

3. Faraday's motor was just a simple demonstration, but it laid the foundation for all the electric motors that followed. It showed that electricity and magnetism could be used to create motion.

4. In 1831, Faraday made another important discovery. He found that moving a magnet near a coil of wire could generate an electric current in the wire. This is the basic principle behind generators and transformers.

5. In 1832, a French instrument maker named Hippolyte Pixii built the first practical generator using Faraday's principles. It used a rotating magnet to generate alternating current (AC) electricity.

6. In 1834, a German mathematician named Moritz Jacobi created the first practical electric motor. It used an electromagnet to rotate a shaft and could lift a weight of 10 to 12 pounds.

7. In 1837, an American blacksmith named Thomas Davenport patented the first electric motor in the United States. He used it to power a small model train, which he displayed at fairs and exhibitions.

8. In 1873, a Belgian electrical engineer named Zénobe Gramme invented the first practical DC motor. It used a ring-shaped armature and a commutator to convert AC electricity into DC electricity.

9. Gramme's motor was more efficient and powerful than earlier designs. It quickly became popular in industries like printing, where it was used to power printing presses and other machinery.

10. In 1887, the American inventor Nikola Tesla developed the first AC motor. Unlike DC motors, which used brushes and commutators, Tesla's motor used rotating magnetic fields to create motion.

11. Tesla's AC motor was more efficient and reliable than DC motors. It also allowed electricity to be transmitted over long distances, which made it possible to power factories and homes far from power plants.

12. In 1888, the American industrialist George Westinghouse bought the rights to Tesla's patents and began manufacturing AC motors and generators. This helped to standardize the use of AC electricity in the United States.

13. In the early 1900s, electric motors began to replace steam engines in factories and other industrial settings. They were more efficient, cleaner, and easier to control than steam engines.

14. During World War I, electric motors were used to power ships, tanks, and aircraft. They allowed these vehicles to move faster and more efficiently than ever before.

15. In the 1920s and 1930s, electric motors began to be used in a wide range of household appliances, including vacuum cleaners, washing machines, and refrigerators. This made daily life easier and more convenient for millions of people.

16. During World War II, electric motors were used in a variety of military applications, including radar systems, anti-aircraft guns, and torpedoes. They helped to give the Allies a technological advantage over the Axis powers.

17. In the 1950s and 1960s, the development of solid-state electronics led to smaller and more powerful electric motors. These motors were used in everything from computer hard drives to space satellites.

18. Today, electric motors are used in a wide range of applications, from electric cars and robots to wind turbines and medical devices. They continue to play a vital role in our daily lives and in the global economy.

19. The development of the electric motor has also had a profound impact on the environment. By replacing steam engines and other fossil fuel-powered machines, electric motors have helped to reduce air pollution and greenhouse gas emissions.

20. As we look to the future, the electric motor will continue to play a vital role in our lives. From powering renewable energy systems to enabling new forms of transportation and automation, the possibilities are endless. The story of the electric motor is a testament to the power of human ingenuity and the importance of scientific discovery.

Chapter 23: The story behind the first submarine

1. The idea of traveling underwater has fascinated people for centuries. In ancient times, divers used hollow reeds to breathe underwater, but it wasn't until the 16th century that the first submarine was invented.

2. In 1578, an English mathematician named William Bourne designed a wooden submarine that could be submerged and rowed underwater. However, it was never built.

3. In 1620, a Dutch inventor named Cornelis Drebbel built a wooden submarine that could hold 12 rowers and stay submerged for several hours. It was tested in the Thames River in London.

4. In 1776, during the American Revolutionary War, a Yale student named David Bushnell built a one-man submarine called the "Turtle." It was used in an unsuccessful attempt to attach explosives to British ships.

5. In 1800, an American inventor named Robert Fulton designed a submarine called the "Nautilus." It used a hand-cranked propeller to move through the water and could stay submerged for up to six hours.

6. In 1864, during the American Civil War, the Confederate Navy built a submarine called the "H.L. Hunley." It sank a Union ship but was also lost at sea, along with its crew of eight.

7. In 1866, a French naval architect named Narcís Monturiol launched the "Ictineo II," a submarine that used a chemical reaction to generate oxygen for the crew. It could dive to depths of up to 30 meters.

8. In 1900, the U.S. Navy bought a submarine designed by the Irish inventor John Philip Holland. It was called the "USS Holland" and was the first submarine to be commissioned by the U.S. Navy.

9. During World War I, submarines played a major role in naval warfare. Germany used submarines, or "U-boats," to sink Allied ships, while the Allies used them to protect their own ships and convoys.

10. In 1922, a German engineer named Hellmuth Walter invented a new type of submarine engine that used hydrogen peroxide as fuel. It allowed submarines to stay submerged for longer periods and travel at higher speeds.

11. During World War II, submarines were used extensively by both the Axis and Allied powers. German U-boats sank thousands of Allied ships, while American submarines helped to cut off Japan's supply lines in the Pacific.

12. In 1954, the U.S. Navy launched the "USS Nautilus," the world's first nuclear-powered submarine. It could stay submerged for months at a time and travel faster and farther than any previous submarine.

13. In 1960, the U.S. Navy launched the "USS Triton," a nuclear-powered submarine that circumnavigated the globe underwater in just 60 days. It was a dramatic demonstration of the capabilities of modern submarines.

14. In 1968, a Soviet submarine called the "K-129" sank in the Pacific Ocean. The U.S. CIA launched a secret mission, called "Project Azorian," to recover the submarine and its nuclear missiles from the ocean floor.

15. In 1986, a Soviet submarine called the "K-219" experienced a catastrophic accident and sank in the Atlantic Ocean. The crew managed to evacuate, but the submarine's nuclear reactor posed a serious environmental threat.

16. Today, submarines are used by navies around the world for a variety of purposes, including intelligence gathering, special operations, and strategic deterrence. They are some of the most advanced and complex machines ever built.

17. Modern submarines can dive to depths of over 1,000 meters and stay submerged for months at a time. They use advanced sonar systems to navigate and detect other ships and submarines.

18. Some of the largest submarines in the world are the Russian "Typhoon" class submarines, which are over 170 meters long and can carry up to 20 nuclear missiles. They are designed to operate under the Arctic ice cap.

19. Despite their capabilities, submarines can be dangerous places to work. Crews must be highly trained and able to handle the physical and psychological challenges of living and working in a confined space for long periods.

20. The story of the submarine is a story of human ingenuity and perseverance. From the early wooden boats of the 16th century to the nuclear-powered behemoths of today, submarines have pushed the boundaries of what is possible and have changed the course of history. They are a testament to the power of science, engineering, and the human spirit.

Chapter 24: The invention of the radio

1. Long ago, people could only communicate with each other by sending letters or messages through telegraph wires. But then, in the late 1800s, a new invention changed everything: the radio.

2. The radio was invented by a young Italian man named Guglielmo Marconi. When he was just 20 years old, Marconi became fascinated with the idea of sending messages through the air without wires.

3. Marconi experimented with different ways of transmitting signals, using a spark gap transmitter and an antenna. In 1895, he successfully sent a radio signal over a distance of about a mile.

4. Other inventors, including Nikola Tesla and Alexander Popov, were also working on ways to transmit signals wirelessly. But Marconi was the first to develop a practical and reliable radio system.

5. In 1897, Marconi founded the Wireless Telegraph and Signal Company in England. He began building radio stations and demonstrating his invention to the public.

6. One of Marconi's most famous demonstrations took place in 1901, when he successfully sent a radio signal across the Atlantic Ocean from England to Newfoundland. This was a distance of over 2,000 miles!

7. The first radio broadcast took place on Christmas Eve, 1906, when a Canadian inventor named Reginald Fessenden played music and read from the Bible over the airwaves. This was the first time that sound had been transmitted by radio.

8. During World War I, the radio became an important tool for military communication. Soldiers used radios to send messages and coordinate attacks, while civilians used them to stay informed about the war.

9. After the war, radio broadcasting began to take off as a form of entertainment. In the 1920s, radio stations began popping up all over the United States and Europe, playing music, news, and other programs.

10. One of the most famous radio broadcasts of all time took place in 1938, when Orson Welles and the Mercury Theatre on the Air performed a dramatic adaptation of the science fiction novel "The War of the Worlds." Many listeners believed that the broadcast was a real news report about an alien invasion!

11. During World War II, the radio played a crucial role in keeping people informed and boosting morale. Governments used radio to broadcast propaganda and news updates, while soldiers listened to radio programs for entertainment and to stay connected with home.

12. In the 1950s and 60s, the rise of television began to challenge the dominance of radio. But radio adapted by focusing on music, talk shows, and local news and weather reports.

13. One of the most important developments in radio technology was the invention of the transistor in 1947. This tiny device allowed radios to become much smaller and more portable, leading to the development of handheld radios and even car radios.

14. In the 1960s and 70s, radio played a key role in the rise of rock and roll music. Disc jockeys like Alan Freed and Wolfman Jack became cultural icons, introducing listeners to new artists and sounds.

15. Radio has also been used for important social and political purposes. During the civil rights movement of the 1960s, African American activists used radio to organize protests and spread their message of equality.

16. In 1977, the Voyager 1 and 2 spacecraft were launched with a special "Golden Record" onboard, containing sounds and images from Earth. The record includes greetings in 55 different languages, as well as music and other audio recordings, all transmitted using radio waves.

17. Today, radio remains an important medium for communication and entertainment around the world. It has evolved to include digital and satellite radio, as well as online streaming services.

18. In developing countries, radio is often the most accessible and affordable form of media. It is used to provide education, health information, and other important services to remote and underserved communities.

19. Radio has also played a role in scientific research. In the 1930s, a young radio astronomer named Karl Jansky discovered radio waves coming from the center of the Milky Way galaxy, opening up a new field of study called radio astronomy.

20. The invention of the radio has had a profound impact on the world. It has connected people across vast distances, provided entertainment and education, and played a crucial role in some of the most important events of the 20th century. From Marconi's first experiments to the digital age, the story of radio is a testament

to the power of human ingenuity and the enduring importance of communication.

Chapter 25: The creation of the rocket

1. Long ago, people dreamed of flying to the stars. They looked up at the night sky and wondered what lay beyond the Earth. But it wasn't until the 20th century that the first rockets were invented, making space travel possible.

2. The idea of using rockets to travel through space has been around for centuries. In the 2nd century CE, a Greek mathematician named Hero of Alexandria designed a simple rocket that used steam to spin a sphere.

3. In the 13th century, a Chinese inventor named Wan Hu tried to launch himself into space using a chair with 47 rockets attached. According to legend, the rockets exploded and Wan Hu was never seen again.

4. In the late 19th and early 20th centuries, pioneers like Konstantin Tsiolkovsky, Robert Goddard, and Hermann Oberth began to develop the mathematical and scientific principles behind modern rocketry.

5. In 1926, Robert Goddard launched the first liquid-fueled rocket in Auburn, Massachusetts. The rocket flew for just 2.5 seconds and reached a height of 41 feet, but it was a major breakthrough in rocket technology.

6. During World War II, rockets were used as weapons by both the Axis and Allied powers. Germany developed the V-2 rocket, which was used to bomb London and other cities.

7. After the war, the United States and the Soviet Union began a "Space Race" to develop more advanced rockets and launch satellites and humans into space.

8. In 1957, the Soviet Union launched the first artificial satellite, Sputnik 1, into orbit using a rocket called the R-7. This event shocked the United States and sparked a new wave of investment in rocket technology.

9. In 1961, Soviet cosmonaut Yuri Gagarin became the first human to orbit the Earth, traveling in a spacecraft called Vostok 1. His flight lasted just over an hour and made him an international celebrity.

10. In 1969, American astronauts Neil Armstrong and Buzz Aldrin became the first humans to walk on the moon, traveling in a spacecraft called Apollo 11. Their mission was powered by the Saturn V rocket, which remains the most powerful rocket ever built.

11. In the 1970s and 80s, the United States developed the Space Shuttle program, which used reusable rockets to launch astronauts and payloads into orbit. The first Space Shuttle, Columbia, launched in 1981.

12. In the 1990s and 2000s, new countries and private companies began to enter the space race. Japan, China, and India all launched their own rockets and satellites, while companies like SpaceX and Blue Origin began developing reusable rockets.

13. One of the most ambitious rocket projects in recent years has been NASA's Space Launch System (SLS), which is designed to carry astronauts and cargo to the moon and eventually to Mars. The first test flight of the SLS is scheduled for 2021.

14. Rockets have also been used to study the Earth and other planets in our solar system. NASA's Voyager 1 and 2 spacecraft, launched in 1977, have traveled farther than any other human-made object and are still sending back data from interstellar space.

15. In addition to exploring space, rockets have also been used for more practical purposes, such as launching satellites for communication, navigation, and weather forecasting. Today, there are over 2,000 active satellites orbiting the Earth.

16. One of the biggest challenges in rocket science is dealing with the extreme temperatures and pressures involved in space travel. Rockets must be designed to withstand temperatures ranging from -450°F to 5,000°F and pressures up to 200 times that of Earth's atmosphere.

17. Another challenge is the cost of building and launching rockets. The Saturn V rocket used for the Apollo missions cost over $6 billion in today's dollars, while the Space Shuttle program cost an estimated $209 billion over its lifetime.

18. Despite the challenges, the future of space exploration looks bright. Private companies like SpaceX and Blue Origin are developing new technologies to make rockets more affordable and reusable, while NASA and other space agencies are planning missions to the moon, Mars, and beyond.

19. One of the most exciting prospects for the future of rocketry is the possibility of using rockets to establish permanent human settlements on other worlds. Some scientists and entrepreneurs envision a future where humans live and work on the moon, Mars, and even more distant planets.

20. The story of the rocket is a story of human curiosity, ingenuity, and perseverance. From the earliest dreams of flying to the stars to the latest missions to explore the universe, rockets have opened up new frontiers and expanded our understanding of the cosmos. As we continue to reach for the stars, the future of rocketry is sure to be filled with new discoveries and adventures.

Conclusion

As we've seen throughout this incredible journey, the world of invention is full of surprises, twists, and turns. From the accidental discovery of the microwave oven to the life-changing impact of the printing press, each story in this book has taught us something new about the power of human curiosity and the endless possibilities of science and technology.

But the best part? The journey doesn't end here. Every day, inventors around the world are working on new ideas and technologies that could change our lives in ways we never thought possible. Who knows what incredible inventions the future might hold? Maybe you'll be the one to invent the next big thing!

So keep exploring, keep learning, and keep dreaming big. The world of invention is full of opportunities, and there's no limit to what you can achieve with a little creativity and a lot of determination. Who knows? Maybe someday, your name will be in a book like this one, inspiring a new generation of young inventors to follow in your footsteps. The future is in your hands – what will you create?

Printed in Great Britain
by Amazon